Captain AWESOME

and the EASTER EGG BANDIT

By STAN KIRBY

Illustrated by GEORGE O'CONNOR

LITTLE SIMON

New York   London   Toronto   Sydney   New Delhi

LITTLE SIMON
An imprint of Simon & Schuster Children's Publishing Division • 1230 Avenue of the Americas, New York, New York 10020 • First Little Simon paperback edition January 2015 • Copyright © 2015 by Simon & Schuster, Inc. All rights reserved, including the right of reproduction in whole or in part in any form. LITTLE SIMON is a registered trademark of Simon & Schuster, Inc., and associated colophon is a trademark of Simon & Schuster, Inc. For information about special discounts for bulk purchases, please contact Simon & Schuster Special Sales at 1-866-506-1949 or business@simonandschuster.com. The Simon & Schuster Speakers Bureau can bring authors to your live event. For more information or to book an event contact the Simon & Schuster Speakers Bureau at 1-866-248-3049 or visit our website at www.simonspeakers.com. Designed by Jay Colvin.
Manufactured in the United States of America 1114 FFG 2 4 6 8 10 9 7 5 3 1
Library of Congress Cataloging-in-Publication Data • Kirby, Stan. Captain Awesome and the Easter egg bandit / by Stan Kirby ; illustrated by George O'Connor. — First edition. pages cm. — (Captain Awesome ; 13) Summary: When their classmates' decorated Easter eggs go missing, Eugene and his friends turn into Captain Awesome and the Sunnyview Superhero Squad and pursue a supervillain. [1. Superheroes—Fiction. 2. Easter eggs—Fiction. 3. Schools—Fiction.] I. O'Connor, George, illustrator. II. Title. PZ7.K633529Cab 2015 [Fic]—dc23 2014006272
ISBN 978-1-4814-2559-9 (hc)
ISBN 978-1-4814-2558-2 (pbk)
ISBN 978-1-4814-2560-5 (eBook)

Table of Contents

1. An Egg-stra Special Day!................................. 1

2. Blue-Pen Blues.. 15

3. The Thumper... 25

4. Superhero Senses.. 35

5. Whodunit?... 45

6. The Scene of the Crime................................. 61

7. Agents of STINK.. 73

8. Here Comes Peter Rotten Tail........................... 83

9. When Turbo Squeaks...................................... 93

10. A MI-TEE Easter Egg Hunt.............................. 105

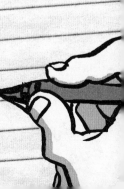

CHAPTER 1

An Egg-stra Special Day!

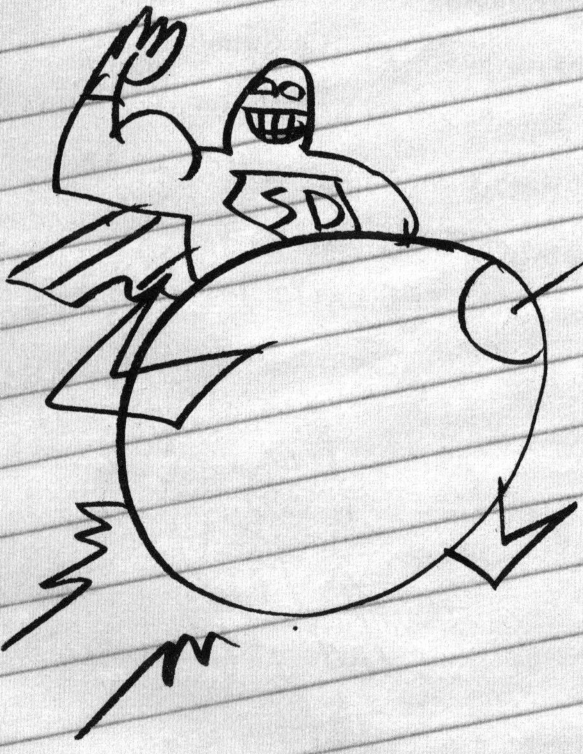

By Eugene

Mission Control, this is *Eggle*-1, do you read me? Over," said Eugene McGillicudy. He picked up a plastic egg from his desk and carried it around the room. "We're now flying over Sunnyview Elementary. . . . Roger that, Roger."

"That's so not the way to decorate an Easter egg," said Meredith Mooney, the pinkest girl in school. She was dressed in a pink skirt

that matched the pink bow in her hair. Her light pink shirt matched her light pink shoes that blinked with pink lights on the toes. "What is that supposed to be, anyway?" she asked.

"If you must know—My! Me! Mine! Mere-DITH! It's *Eggle*-1,"

Eugene said. "It is a ship that carries egg-stronauts to the twelve slots on the orbiting Space Carton."

"Oh, good grief," Meredith said with a groan.

She went back to coloring her own eggs in different shades of pink.

With only four days until Easter, Ms. Beasley's class was decorating eggs. Wilma Eisner and

Betty Alfa worked as a team, each painting half of each other's eggs. Gil Ditko was off in the corner working in secret. Dara Sim was busy painting her eggs black. Evan Mason was gluing two eggs together to make a superegg.

Ms. Beasley walked around the class, checking the work of each student. "That's good," she said. "Very interesting, Dara. That's . . . unique, Evan. Meredith, I see you're staying with pink."

"Is there any other color worth

coloring eggs with, Ms. Beasley?"
Meredith asked.

"Check this out,
Ms. Beasley!"
Eugene cut
in. He held
up an egg. It
had a tiny
blue door
painted on
it. "I call
it Eggtopia.
It's where the tiny Egg People live,
safe from the deadly Maple Bacon
Warlords."

Ms. Beasley smiled and quickly moved away.

She likes it! thought Eugene.

Eugene dipped his brush into green paint and painted a zigzag onto his egg. "And that's the control panel for the force field."

Eugene got the name Eggtopia from that time Super Dude fought against the evil Easter Boney, the skeleton pirate in Super Dude's Holiday Egg-stravaganza No. 3.

What's that, you say? You haven't heard of Super Dude, the world's mightiest superhero?

Are you a stranger to this planet? Do you live in a world surrounded by an eggshell? Super Dude is just the greatest comic book superhero ever!

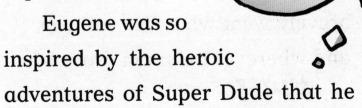

Eugene was so inspired by the heroic adventures of Super Dude that he

made his own superhero suit. When he put it on, he became Captain Awesome. Captain Awesome bravely went wherever evil was . . . and wherever his mom drove him.

MI-TEE!

Eugene's best friend, Charlie Thomas Jones, was also a big fan of Super Dude. He became Nacho Cheese Man, the only hero with the power of canned cheese. **CHEESY-YO!**

The last to join their team was Sally Williams. Dressed as Super-sonic Sal, she was lightning fast! Her sidekick, Funny Cat, was pretty cool too.

SPEEDY GO!

Together these three heroes and the class hamster, known only as Turbo, formed the Sunnyview Superhero Squad.

SQUAD UP!

But for now, there was no evil in Ms. Beasley's class.

CHAPTER 2

Blue-Pen Blues

By
Eugene

Eugene shoved Eggtopia in front of Charlie.

"Check it out, Charlie," Eugene said. "I bet people from all over the world will come to see my super spectacular egg art pieces. Museums will fight one another just to put a Captain Awesome original on display."

"Maybe they will want mine, too!" Charlie said. He was painting

an egg bright yellow with dark spots.
"It's the Swiss Twister. Inside, I have
hidden several squares of excellent
cheese." He twisted the plastic egg
and took out a cube of Swiss. "Deli-
cious."

Sally held out her own egg.

It was bright blue
with a large gold
lightning bolt.
"I call mine
the Yolk of
Justice," she
said proudly.

Eugene
went back to his
seat. He reached
into his desk for his
blue Super Dude Super Marking
Pen to sign his name on the bottom
of his eggs. His hand felt nothing but
the spiral binding of his notebook.

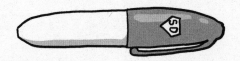

He looked into the desk. Nothing.

My Super Dude Super Marking Pen is gone!

It was just like that time in Super Dude No. 219, when the evil Crayonosaurus Rex tried to steal all the markers so he could control the world's color. That was definitely a job for Super Dude. This

was a job for Captain Awesome!

Eugene's backpack with his Captain Awesome costume was

back in his cubby. He'd have to sneak over there without anyone seeing. Eugene dropped to his hands and knees. He quickly crawled down the rows to his cubby.

SUCCESS!

Eugene grabbed his backpack. He was just seconds away from becoming Captain Awesome. Then

he'd discover what evil person, villain, or thing had stolen his blue pen.

"Eugene McGillicudy! Please take your seat," Ms. Beasley said. She was always saying that.

"Yes, ma'am." Eugene slumped back to his desk.

As soon as

he plopped down, Eugene felt a tap on his shoulder.

Charlie handed Eugene the blue pen. "Thanks for letting me borrow this!" he said. "It writes really well!"

Charlie held up his egg with his name scrawled on the bottom.

"Oh! Um. No problem," Eugene mumbled.

Another case solved!

CHAPTER 3

The Thumper

By
Eugene

They're . . . Well, they're awesome!" Eugene said to his parents. "They are the greatest Easter eggs you've ever seen."

Eugene popped a long strand of spaghetti into his mouth and slurped it up. The end whipped so fast that it tapped his nose.

"One is a space shuttle. Another has a whole city inside. And then I made another one . . . and—"

"WAHHH!" Eugene's baby sister, Molly, screamed. She threw her spoon on the floor.

"One second," Eugene's dad said. He got up to get Molly a new spoon.

Eugene leaned in close in case the house was bugged. "I gave it razor-sharp teeth and fins. It's called the Egg White Shark!"

"BLAAAH!" Molly smeared tomato sauce on her cheek.

"Excuse me." Eugene's mom went to get a napkin to wipe Molly's messy face.

Up. Down. Up. Down. That was all his parents did. Every time Molly opened her mouth.

YIKES!

That was when it hit Eugene like the meatball Molly had just thrown across the table. This was an evil plan to ruin his dinner.

Captain Awesome's stinky nemesis had returned. It was Queen Stinkypants from Planet Baby!

With her evil babbling, terrible tantrums, and—*PEW!*—stinky dia-pers, she was turning his parents into mindless zombies. They were being forced to give her everything she wanted!

His mother returned with a surprise.

"I was saving this for your

Easter gift," she said to Queen Stinkypants. "But this seems like a better time for it." After her daughter's face was clean, Betsy handed Queen Stinkypants a big, pink stuffed rabbit.

Queen Stinkypants said something that sounded like "Earthling good!" She gave the bunny a big hug. Then started to chew on its left ear, infecting it with her awful Stinkydrool.

Eugene did not like the look of this bunny. There was something about those beady black eyes.

"Nom-nom-nom . . ." Queen Stinkypants gnawed at the toy's ear. Then she lifted the bunny above her head and thumped him down on her high chair.

The sound filled Eugene with horror. It was THE THUMPER. Captain Awesome would have to add another villain to his list of "Villains to Fight." And this one was a big pink bunny with drool-germs in its fur.

Eugene stared at the Thumper. The Thumper stared back. And stared. And stared . . .

CHAPTER 4

Superhero Senses

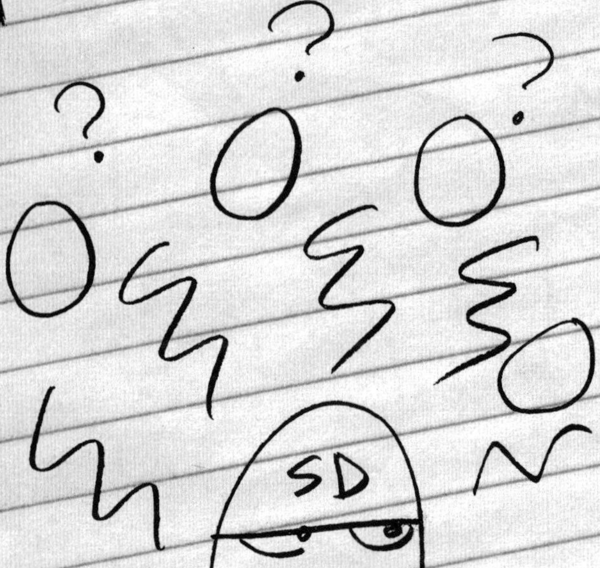

By Eugene

TINGLE!

Eugene felt it the moment he walked into school with Charlie and Sally. It was Thursday: three days before Easter.

DOUBLE TINGLE!

"Did you feel that?"

"Feel what, Eugene?" Sally said.

"I got nothing," Charlie replied.

"That's because you guys don't

have Awesome-Sense like I do," Eugene said.

"I have a Supersonic Sense," Sally said. "And I don't feel anything."

"I can sense cheese." Charlie sniffed. "Someone has pepper jack in their lunch box."

TRIPLE TINGLE!

"There it is again!" Eugene looked around. Where was the danger? Would it be a Scaly Green Martian attack from the ceiling? A Booger-Shooting Locker Dragon from down the hall? Or a Million Zombie Moles from just under the floor?

They entered Ms. Beasley's classroom. Kids were busy putting their backpacks in their cubbies. Others were taking their seats and getting out their papers and pencils to start work.

NORMAL.

Charlie checked the hamster hutch and said good morning to Turbo. "He seems fine, Eugene."

By the time Eugene reached his desk and sat down, he knew

something was horribly wrong. But what?

WHAT?

What was bothering him?

Eugene reached into his desk to pull out his Easter eggs.

NOTHING.

He felt again. And again. He pulled everything out from his desk and bent his head to look inside.

SHOCK!

His Easter eggs were gone!

"Sally! Charlie!" he whispered urgently. "Check your desks!"

"My Easter eggs are gone!" Sally gasped.

"Someone stole our eggs!" Charlie said.

Eugene looked around. The whole classroom had been cleared of the colorful plastic eggs. But nobody else seemed upset.

This was just like Super Dude No. 48, when Super Dude fought Pizzarita. She brainwashed kids into thinking they only liked plain

pizza. Then she stole the pizzas
from the school cafeteria and ate
all the pepperoni.

Eugene eyed his classmates.
This was clearly a case for Cap-
tain Awesome and the Sunnyview
Superhero Squad!

CHAPTER 5

Whodunit?

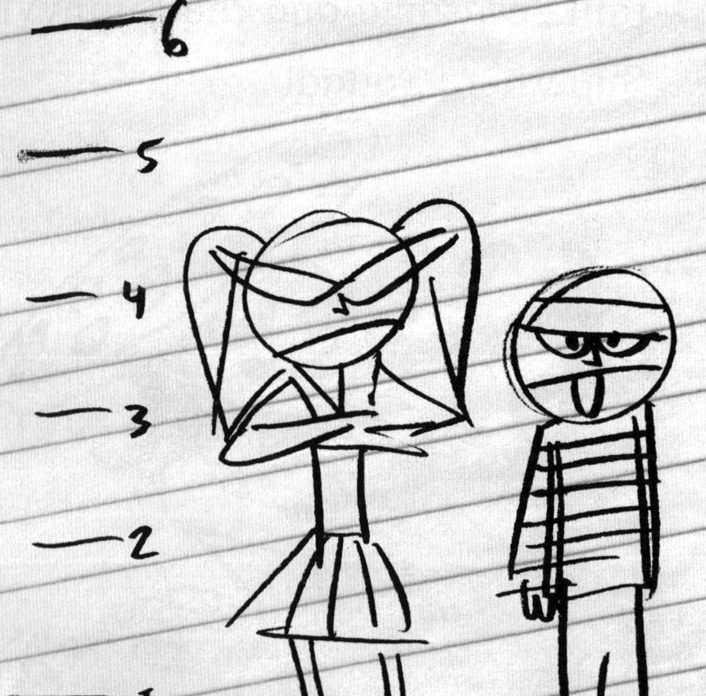

By Eugene

The school bell rang. Eugene watched his classmates run out the door for morning recess. Eugene stayed behind.

"I'll meet you at the supersecret school-time Sunnyview Superhero Squad Clubhouse," he told Sally and Charlie.

Eugene wanted to check the desks of his classmates. Just in case the thief was hiding the eggs nearby.

Just as he was about to start his search, the janitor came in and started sweeping.

"You should get outside," the janitor said. "Get some of that sun-shine. Big tetherball game going on."

SIGH.

Eugene left Ms. Beasley's class. Charlie and Sally waited for him behind the twisty slide, near the big maple tree.

"This emergency meeting of the
Sunnyview Superhero Squad may
now begin," Charlie said.

"Squad, we have a mystery,"
Eugene said. "And with Easter this

weekend, we don't have much time to solve it."

Sally and Charlie nodded. "I've already got a plan," Charlie said. "First, I cover everyone in canned cheese. Then . . . we wait."

Sally and Eugene looked at Charlie. "How does that help us?" Sally asked.

Charlie shrugged.

"Or . . ." Eugene said. "We could watch everyone for weird behavior

during lunch and see what they do. The person who stole our most awe-some eggs won't be able to resist looking at them during the day."

"Well, if you don't want to do things the cheesy way," complained Charlie.

"I predict this crime will be solved by lunch!" Eugene predicted.

It wasn't.

Lunch arrived, and Eugene,
Charlie, and Sally sat at their usual
table, keeping an eye on their classmates.

"I've got Gil," Eugene said. "And
Meredith."

"I've got Dara and Evan," Sally
said.

"I've got a cheese sandwich,"

Charlie said. He squirted some white cheddar onto a piece of bread. "With extra cheese." Charlie looked up from his lunch. "Oh, and Olivia and Jake."

The members of the Sunny-view Superhero Squad decided to split up and snoop. Number six of Super Dude's Ten Rules of Justice was: If you want to know what evil is doing . . . ask it questions.

"What did I do after school yesterday?" Meredith asked. "What is it to you?"

"I'm working on a project for Easter," Eugene lied. "Just to see

what everyone has been doing."

"I went to the mall with my mom," she said. "We did mall stuff, and then none-of-your-business stuff."

"I was watching TV," said Evan.

"Homework," said Dara.

"Ballet," said Olivia.

"Gymnastics," Jake said.

"If you must know," said Gil, "I was secretly plotting to take over the world."

At last! Eugene had found the villain!

"Just kidding," Gil said. "I went to soccer practice."

ARGH!

Eugene, Charlie, and Sally stood in the doorway of the lunchroom. They watched their classmates finish eating. "Each of them has a good excuse," Eugene said.

"None of them could've taken the eggs," Charlie agreed.

"We'll have to look somewhere else," Sally said.

They stopped whispering as Wilma headed toward them. *Has*

she come to confess? wondered Eugene.

"I heard you were asking questions and I didn't want to be left out," Wilma said. "I was at piano lessons!"

She dropped her juice box in the recycling bin and headed back to class.

"Drat!" Eugene said, disappointed.

CHAPTER 6

The Scene of the Crime

DO NOT CROSS

By
Eugene

I know what the problem is! We're looking at this crime as Eugene, Charlie, and Sally. We should be looking at this as the superheroes we really are," said Eugene.

"To the costumes!" Charlie shouted.

The trio raced down the hallway toward Ms. Beasley's classroom.

BACKPACKS!

UNZIP!
CAPE!
SUPERHEROES!

Captain Awesome guessed they had ten minutes before lunch was over. That should be plenty of

time for the Sunnyview Superhero
Squad to search their classroom
for clues.

"I'll bet whoever stole the
Easter eggs is making them into

scrambled eggs right now." Nacho
Cheese Man sighed. "Or worse:
hard-boiled eggs!"

"We're not going to give up . . . ,"
Captain Awesome began. "Things
may look bad, but did Super Dude

give up when the Cyborg Chickens from the future sent the Eggs-Terminator back in time to steal his superpowers?! No, he did not! And neither will we!"

"We are with you, Captain Awesome!" Supersonic Sal said. "What's the plan?"

But before Captain Awesome could say another word, he saw it! There, on the wall in the hallway . . .

A SHADOW!

And not just any shadow, but the bunny ears of the dreaded villain, the Thumper!

"I should have known that furball was the egg bandit!" Captain Awesome said. "Hop to it, guys! Quick! Before he gets away!"

The three heroes ran into the hall and struck their

most heroic poses, ready for an all-out fuzzy bunny battle! But instead of a fur-rocious supervillain, the Sunnyview Superhero Squad came face-to-face with . . .

Ms. Beasley?!

"Oh!" Ms. Beasley said. She was startled by the sudden appearance of Captain Awesome, Supersonic Sal, and Nacho Cheese Man. She quickly slipped something into her purse. "I thought everyone was eating lunch."

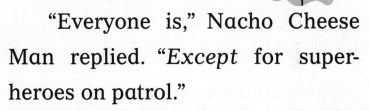

"Everyone is," Nacho Cheese Man replied. "*Except* for super-heroes on patrol."

"Have you noticed anything weird going on?" Supersonic Sal asked.

"Weird?" Ms. Beasley replied,
looking at the superheroes.

"Yeah, like a furry supervillain
trying to steal all the Easter eggs in
the world," Captain Awesome said.

"That *is* weird," Ms. Beasley replied. "If I *do* see something like that going on, I will *certainly* let you know."

"Good! And whatever you do, don't eat any scrambled eggs," Nacho Cheese Man said. "They could be evidence!"

"Good thing I already had breakfast," Ms. Beasley said.

Agents of STINK

By
Eugene

At home, after school, Eugene crept down the hall. One false move could set off the Stinkypants Alarm. Then things could really get smelly.

He tiptoed into Queen Stinkypants's Fortress of Stinkitude and peeked inside.

SNIFF! SNIFF!

It didn't smell *too* bad. Queen Stinkypants was gone. But she hadn't left her Fortress of Stinkitude unguarded!

The Thumper sat at a small table with a tea set. The rest of Queen Stinkypants's evil Agents of STINK sat with him: Smelly the Bear! The Stink Fairy! Princess PU! They were probably plotting some evil plan to

stink up the whole world!

Eugene sat down across from his number-one suspect. "I'm on to you," Eugene said. "My parents may have fallen for your soft pink fur and cute fuzzy ears, but I know you're stuffed with evil! Tell me where you hid the Easter eggs!"

The Thumper stared silently at Eugene. And stared. And stared. And *stared*. He didn't blink. He *never* blinked.

"Giving me the silent treatment, huh?" Eugene asked. "Well, you may have won this round, but I *will* get those eggs back!"

"Now, isn't that the sweetest thing ever?" said a voice from behind him.

UH-OH.

Eugene spun around. His mom and Queen Stinkypants stood in the doorway. Eugene threw a quick look back to the Thumper. "So that's your game, huh? Distract me long enough

for your boss, Queen Stinkypants,
to launch a surprise diaper attack!"

"Eugene, you are *so* cute playing tea with Molly's dolls," Eugene's
mom said.

"Dolls? You mean the Agents of STINK!" Eugene replied. "And I'm not playing tea with anyone!"

"This will make the *cutest* picture. Go on, Molly, sit next to your brother." Eugene's mom nudged Molly forward.

"Gaaaa gooo bwaaaaa maaaa paaaaap!" Molly waddled over to Eugene. She plopped down at the

table and began to drool on her plastic fairy. Eugene could smell the terrible stink of her stinky stink powers.

"Moooom!" Eugene said, groaning.

"Smile!" said Eugene's mom. She ignored her son's protests and took a photo with her phone.

CLICK!

"This really stinks!" Eugene complained.

Eugene's mom sniffed the air.

"I think that's Molly's diaper. I'll change your sister. You go comb your hair."

SHOCK!

HORROR!

"Comb my hair?!" Eugene gasped. "But I didn't do anything wrong!"

"I'm not punishing you, silly. We're going to the mall to take Easter pictures."

It was then that he realized the horrible truth. His mom's brain had been removed and replaced with one of Queen Stinkypants's diapers! His mom was now a diaper-brained mind monkey!

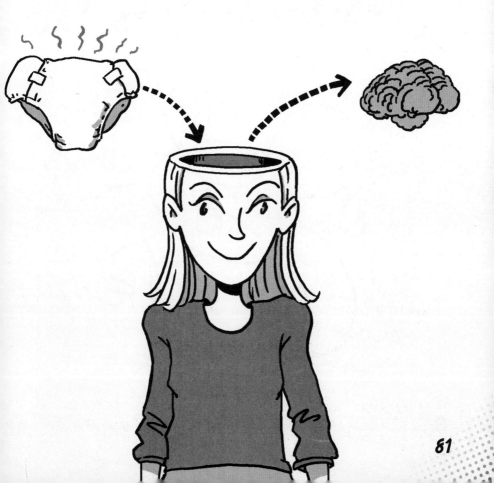

CHAPTER 8

Here Comes Peter Rotten Tail

By
Eugene

Mom, we've been standing in this line for infinity plus one. How much longer do we have to wait?" Eugene tugged at the itchy collar of his nice shirt.

"It's almost our turn," Eugene's mom replied. "Why can't you be patient like your little sister?"

"Gooo!" Molly blurted. She stuck Princess PU's head in her mouth.

Eugene stood on his tiptoes and tried to see what was at the front of the line. Then he saw it. It was the most evil of holiday-themed super-villains! It was worse than Santa Claws! Worse than New Year's Evilboy!

It was the egg-stremely awful PETER ROTTEN TAIL.

Peter Rotten Tail had clearly kidnapped the Easter Bunny and now sat on the rabbit throne. He was surrounded by giant baskets of stuffed bunny guards that looked exactly like the Thumper.

"He's cloning bad guys!" Eugene
gasped.

Peter Rotten Tail had long whiskers and even longer bunny ears. He was covered in fuzzy fur, and wore a pink bow tie. You could tell Peter Rotten Tail everything you wanted for Easter, and all you'd get was a smelly sock full of belly-button lint.

Where was the real Easter Bunny?

Eugene looked at the line of people waiting for Peter Rotten Tail. All of them were dressed up in lame clothes with buttons. Their hair

was combed, and they were ready to have their pictures taken with this fake!

Could Peter Rotten Tail's plan be any more evil?!

The answer was "NO!"

Everything finally made sense!

The Thumper wasn't working for
Queen Stinkypants. He was a secret
double agent working
for Peter Rotten
Tail! Queen
Stinkypants
didn't steal
his mom's
brain and
replace it
with a diaper.
Peter Rotten Tail
stole his mom's brain and replaced
it with moldy carrots!

And who knew what he'd done

to the real Easter Bunny?

"I'm on to you, you mean fur-ball!" Eugene shouted. "I'll never let you get away with those stolen Easter eggs!"

"Oh no!" Eugene's mom gasped.

"MI-TEEE!" Captain Awesome shouted as he dove into the huge pile of stuffed rabbits. The other kids standing in line thought that this looked like fun. Soon they

were jumping out of line and into the baskets of stuffed bunnies too. Their laughter and shrieks filled the mall.

Every parent in line turned and glared at Eugene's mom.

CHAPTER 9

When Turbo Squeaks

By
Eugene

Moldy carrots, Eugene? Really?" his mom asked for the fourth time as they drove home. Or maybe the fifth. Eugene had lost count.

"All I wanted was one nice picture of you and your sister to send to Grandma and Grandpa. Is that too much to ask?" Eugene's mom continued.

"No." Eugene sighed. *Unless it's*

a photo with someone who is pure evil and likes to steal Easter eggs, he thought to himself.

"How did it go?" Eugene's dad asked as soon as they came through the door.

Eugene simply sighed loudly. He went straight up to his bedroom. As Captain Awesome, he had *almost* captured the evil Peter Rotten Tail.

"Now I know how Super Dude felt when the Human Rain Cloud rained on the Super Dude Parade," Eugene said.

Eugene had failed. Whatever the opposite of Mi-Tee was, that was exactly how he felt right then.

"EeT-iM," Eugene thought out loud. "That's about as opposite of Mi-Tee as you can get."

Eugene looked around his room. *What now?* he thought. *How do I catch a bad guy who can't be caught?*

Eugene fell back onto his Super Dude pillow, and stared at his Super Dude poster. He closed his eyes. *Just for a minute,* he thought. *Really.*

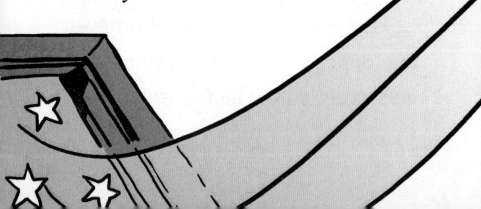

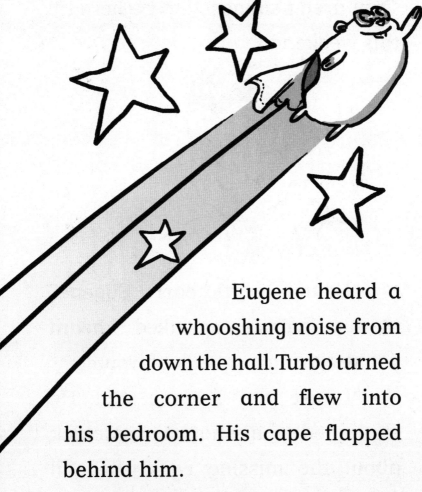

Eugene heard a whooshing noise from down the hall. Turbo turned the corner and flew into his bedroom. His cape flapped behind him.

"Turbo!" Eugene called out.

"You aren't supposed to be here till this weekend!"

"I came a little early, Eugene," the superhamster squeaked. "I heard you're having a squeak of trouble."

"I sure am," Eugene said. He explained to his hamster sidekick about the missing eggs, the evil bunnies, the mall, and everything else. He described how he had almost caught Peter Rotten Tail. "I

was so close!" he said. "But that guy must have a lucky rabbit's foot . . . or maybe four." Eugene sighed.

It was then that Turbo said the Words of Justice that only a flying hamster could say. "The power of many is stronger than the power of one."

For a hamster, Turbo sure knew a lot.

Eugene repeated Turbo's words. "'The power of many is stronger than the power of one.'"

"EUGENE! IT'S DINNERTIME!" Eugene's mom yelled from downstairs.

Dinner already? Eugene rubbed the sleep from his eyes and looked around. Turbo was gone. It had all been a dream.

But what a dream! Eugene thought. Turbo had given him the answer.

He jumped from his bed. Energy raced through his body! He had "the many." He knew "the many." The Sunnyview Superhero Squad was bigger and better than Peter Rotten Tail! Together they were going to find those missing eggs!

"We *WILL* beat the bad guys!" Eugene cheered. *Rumble-gurgle* his stomach growled in agreement.

CHAPTER 10

A MI-TEE
Easter Egg Hunt

By
Eugene

I know who really stole the Easter eggs!" Eugene told Charlie and Sally before class started. "But it will take all of us to stop him!"

"Was it the Egg-bominable Egg-man?" Charlie asked.

"Or the Hen of Doom?" Sally guessed.

"No. Worse than all of them put together times fifty jillion. It was Peter Rotten Tail!" Eugene replied.

"I knew it!" Charlie gasped. Then he added, "Wait, who's Peter Rotten Tail?"

"Only the most horrible villain of the holidays!" Eugene replied. "He's the one who sets up his bad guy headquarters at the mall and makes kids comb their hair and dress in scratchy clothes!"

Charlie nodded. "And he smells like old peas. . . ."

"So, what's the plan?" Sally

asked. "A supersecret Sunnyview Superhero Squad strike on the mall?! If it is, I'll need to ask my mom's permission first."

"We can't do that," Eugene replied.

"Because Peter Rotten Tail's headquarters are too guarded?" Sally asked.

"No. Because mall security

banned me for a month. Again," Eugene explained.

"Could I please have everyone's attention?" Ms. Beasley said, cutting off Eugene. "I have some very exciting news for you."

"I love very exciting news!"

Charlie gasped and spun around in his chair to face Ms. Beasley.

"Some of you may have noticed that your Easter eggs went missing yesterday . . . ," Ms. Beasley began.

"And I know who did it!" Eugene cried, jumping from his chair. "It was Peter Rotten Tail! He wants to make a mountain of scrambled eggs to feed his evil rabbit army! I had the villain

in my grasp"—Eugene clenched his fists—"but a security guard made me leave the mall empty-handed."

Ms. Beasley stood silent and blinked several times.

"No, Eugene. Peter, um, Rotten Tail, was it? He didn't take the Easter eggs," Ms. Beasley explained.

"But— But— But—" Eugene stammered. "He *had* to be the one who stole the Easter eggs. He has a secret undercover spy working for him. The Thumper! You should see his dark eyes . . . staring . . . always *staring*. . . ."

Meredith rolled her eyes. "Sit *down*, Eugerm. No one cares about your underwear agent," she said.

"Under*cover* agent," Eugene corrected her.

"The reason I know that Peter Rotten Tail didn't take away the Easter eggs," Ms. Beasley continued, "is because . . . I did!" Suddenly the teacher whipped out a pair of fake bunny ears and put them on her head.

"SAY WHAAAAAAAAAAT?!" Charlie gasped.

Everything fell into place for Eugene. The shadow on the wall was Ms. Beasley wearing bunny ears. She was the one he had seen in the classroom yesterday. But why did she take the Easter eggs? Why?

WHY?! The question remained.

"In case you're wondering why I took the Easter eggs, it was to set up a surprise Easter egg hunt for everyone!" Ms. Beasley explained.

Ooooooh. That's why, Eugene thought. The classroom erupted into cheers of joy.

Ms. Beasley handed out Easter baskets. The kids raced outside to the schoolyard for the Easter egg hunt.

"I hope you're not too disappointed it's just a plain old Easter egg hunt instead of a supervillain's evil plan," Ms. Beasley said to

Eugene. She handed him a basket.

"Actually . . . fighting bad guys and saving Easter would have been awesome, but I think an Easter egg hunt is even more awesome!" Eugene replied.

"And way less evil," Charlie added.

"And I'm going to find more than either of you!" Sally said.

Eugene, Charlie, and Sally raced out the door, ready to have the greatest Easter egg hunt in the history of Easter egg hunts. There was only one word that could possibly describe how awesome their day was going to be . . .

MI-TEE!

Keep reading for a sneak peek at the next Captain Awesome adventure!

CAPTAIN AWESOME
GOES TO SUPERHERO CAMP

It's all quiet in the neighborhood, Mom," Eugene said. "Too quiet! Ever since school got out, not a single bad guy has tried to take over Sunnyview."

"Something fun must've happened today," said Mrs. McGillicudy.

"I did see Meredith," Eugene replied. "But it wasn't fun, it was evil.

But even she's leaving town for summer camp. Gross princess camp!"

"Camp sounds like fun," Mrs. McGillicudy said.

"Summer camp should be great, not *pink*!" he said. "There should be crime-fighting tips, gadget labs, and lessons on how to be invisible."

"That would be great," agreed his mom.

"Great? It would be awesome!" Eugene declared. "Heroes from all over would gather. It would be like the ultimate team-up of the Hero

League Society and the Society League of Heroes!"

"I wonder if there is a summer camp like that," his mom thought aloud.

Eugene slowly shook his head.

"Probably not," he said. "But I can dream."